AaBbCcDdEeFfGgHhIiJj

This Book Belongs To:

Gavin

From:

Mommy

Date:

PRINCIPAL KIDD

Book #1

"School Rules!"

By Connie T. Colòn

To –
Gavin Cherney
Happy Reading!
♡
Connie T. Colòn

Foundations, LLC.
Brandon, MS 39047
www.FoundationsBooks.net

Principal Kidd: Book 1, School Rules
by Connie T. Colòn
ISBN: **978-1544667034**
Cover by Connie T. Colòn Copyright © 2017
Edited and Formatted by: Laura Ranger
Copyright 2017© Connie T. Colòn

Published in the United States of America
Worldwide Electronic & Digital Rights
Worldwide English Language Print Rights

"A school run by a kid? There's just one word for it: fun!"
- Jerry Spinelli
Award winning children's book author
Website: www.jerryspinelli.com

"Connie Colon has created a funny and empowering story that every kid (and anyone who ever was a kid) will love."
- Alan Kingsberg
TV Writer - Pokemon, Winx Club, Shining Time Station, Are You Afraid of the Dark?
Website: www.alankingsberg.com

"Kids will not only get a kick out of this outrageously funny story, they'll probably want to become the principal of their schools! Colón has a real talent for writing humor that will keep readers laughing long after they've finished the book."
~ Linda Bozzo
Award-winning Children's Author
Website: www.LindaBozzo.com
Facebook: https://goo.gl/BnEIcd

"What young reader could resist Principal Kidd: School Rules by Connie Travisano Colón, a madcap new series set in a school that features a fast lane in the corridors, a live chicken, and a principal who really "is your pal", because he's the same age as the students?"
- Regina Griffin
Highlights Foundation faculty member, former editor-in-chief at Holiday House, ten years editing at Scholastic and two years at multinational publisher, Egmont USA.

"Gob dash it! Taking over as principal of Eggshell Elementary might present wacky trouble for Oliver Kidd, but it leads to laugh-out-loud fun for the reader. *School Rules* rules!"
- Laurie Calkhoven
Author of *Michael at the Invasion of France, 1943.*
Website: www.lauriecalkhoven.com

Dedication

In honor of my mom, Esther Travisano, who is now my guardian angel in heaven. Thank you for all of your love, the laughter, sharing your love of books, reading and schools—and for telling me that I was meant to be a professional writer.

Table of Contents

Chapter 1 13

Chapter 2 21

Chapter 3 28

Chapter 4 37

Chapter 5 44

Chapter 6 47

Chapter 7 53

Chapter 8 56

Chapter 9 60

Chapter 10 66

Chapter 11 70

Chapter 12 74

About the Author 82

Acknowledgements 83

School Rules Contest 85

Other Foundations Titles 87

Chapter

Oliver's heart raced faster than his feet, as he pedaled like a maniac to get away from the TV reporter. Popping wheelies while turning and twisting to avoid more reporters, he finally skidded to an abrupt stop in the principal's parking spot. A seriously abrupt stop. As in flipping off of the bike and landing on his backpack, like a stunned turtle stuck wrong side up down in its shell. Camera flashes blinded him. Microphones were shoved in his face. *Not* a cool way to start the first day of school.

From his vantage point, Oliver witnessed a small orange beak untying the first reporter's shoe. A white chicken bobbed from around the reporter's feet and headed straight for Oliver. She had a patch of bright fuchsia feathers, and wore a tiny sweater with Eggshell Elementary School's logo – an egg on top of three books.

Oliver sat up and straightened his glasses. "Morning, Chelsea!" He gave her outstretched wing a high-five.

The second Oliver was up on his feet, the reporters rushed in close to him. They yapped a mile a minute, smelling like stinky coffee and yucky oatmeal.

One reporter shouted out, "Did you just take your training wheels off of that bike?"

More questions, more camera flashes, more microphones jutted at his face.

"How will you handle bullies bigger than you?"

"Have you lost all your baby teeth yet?"

Oliver's toaster tart tumbled around in his stomach. "I...um...errr..."

Tall, with shoulders as wide as a dump truck, and a permanent scowl where a smile should be, Vice Principal Dagger marched over and loomed above the crowd.

"Gob dash it, everyone get off school property before I call the police!" Mr. Dagger's bellow created a gust of wind that swirled leaves and chicken feathers in the air.

The crowd became silent but no one budged.

Mr. Dagger hated to be kept waiting. His face turned an angry purple while steam blew out of his ears like a whistling teapot. "*Now!*"

The reporters and photographers all scattered to their vehicles. The one with the untied shoe landed like a welcome mat under the feet of the trampling crowd. As Oliver dashed toward his bike, he was stopped by a sudden and unexpected wedgie.

Chelsea flapped her wings. "Bok! Squawk! Bok!" Clearly, she was not amused that her friend received a wedgie.

Oliver felt another yank to the waistband of the back of his pants, was lifted off the ground and placed back on his feet. He found himself back in the center of the principal's parking space.

"I was talking to them, not *you*, Kidd," said Mr. Dagger. "This is your big day. All eyes will be on you. Hope you're ready."

Oliver gulped. His toaster tart did another tumble. "I...I...I..."

Mr. Dagger shook his head. "Iy, yi, yi."

They all walked toward the front entrance of the two-story red brick school. Mr. Dagger pushed his frown down even lower, with a thumb to each corner of his mouth.

Oliver took his helmet off and finger combed his hair. Chelsea followed suit and smoothed her feathers.

"Glad you got rid of the reporters," said Oliver. "I'm fresh out of fun anecdotes about my accelerated education."

"Well gob dash it, Mr. Child Prodigy, it's not like they can report on our sports programs. After all, the school mascot is that ridiculous chicken, for Pete's sake."

"Bok! Bok! Squawk!" Chelsea left a steaming turd on Mr. Dagger's shiny shoes.

"Holy fudge nuggets! Not my new shoes!" The vice principal shook the poop off into the bushes bordering the lawn.

Oliver picked up Chelsea and held her football style, while groups of kids began to spill out of the school buses. Many of the passing students whispered and murmured while pointing at Oliver.

"Look, that brainiac boy is back."

"That's Oliver Kidd, isn't it?"

"I heard he finished college over the summer."

"Who finished college? The chicken?"

Sporting a long braid, bright floral sundress and a mile-wide smile, fifth-grader April Mae March ran to Oliver. She practically squeezed the air out of him with a hug.

"Ollie-Bear, it *is* you! I heard you were back home."

Before Oliver could answer, brown-skinned, blue-eyed, Tucker Wilson, another fifth-grader and April's best friend, pushed his way over.

"Awesome to see ya, bro!"

Tucker began an elaborate handshake with Oliver that started with a fist-bump and then outstretched fingers right before Tucker spun in a circle. He stood there waiting with his hand out, feeling terrible that Ollie didn't remember the rest of the handshake.

Uh oh. Oliver scratched his head. He looked at Chelsea in his left arm, hoping for a clue. When the bird shrugged her wings, Oliver placed her on the ground. He stayed squatted next to her in an attempt to hide his reddening face.

"You really forgot our handshake? C'mon, like this." Tucker stuck his hand out again. "Up, down, and—"

Like a bolt of lightning, suddenly brightening everything, Oliver remembered and jumped to his feet. "...and all around!"

Both boys twirled in a circle and then high-fived up, high-fived down, knocked elbows, knocked shoulders and ended in a grand finale of a belly bump.

"This is going to be just like old times, being back at Eggshell," said Oliver. "Remember kindergarten here? Those were the days, huh?"

Oliver gazed into space and smiled as his thoughts drifted back to their kindergarten days. He pictured the big room that smelled like glue and crayons, with toys and games everywhere. He remembered a tiny Tucker, wearing a cape and hat, chasing a baby Chelsea chick around the room with his magician's wand.

A pint-sized April Mae, with a thick braid longer than she was tall, was at a table with a toy crystal ball, handing out horoscopes.

Oliver pictured himself back on the beanbag chair reading his favorite Quantum Physics book. He had plunked the huge book down with a thud and stood on it. "Here's a good joke for you. Where does bad light go?"

April Mae, Tucker and Chelsea had gathered closer to listen.

Oliver stood taller. "To a prism!"

They all howled with laughter and hugged him.

Kindergarten Tucker tugged on Oliver's polka dotted tie. "Tell us more jokes, Ollie."

Tug. Tug. Tug.

Present day Tucker tugged on that same polka dotted tie with a laugh. He jolted Oliver out of his kindergarten daydream.

"What's with the fancy duds, Ollie? There's no dress code here."

Oliver looked down to adjust his tie. "Um, it's Mr. Kidd."

Tucker looked around, confused. "Your dad's here? No wonder you look all creeped out, bro."

Vice Principal Dagger stepped closer and motioned to Oliver. "He's talking about himself. You need to call him Mr. Kidd now. Haven't you heard the news?"

"What news?" asked April Mae.

Mr. Dagger lifted one thick eyebrow. "Oliver Kidd is the new principal."

Chapter

As students talked and laughed their way down the front hallway, Oliver pulled April Mae and Tucker aside. They huddled near the door to the main office. Oliver stood between the other two and placed a hand on each of their shoulders.

"Sorry I didn't tell you about the new job myself," said Oliver. "Everything happened so fast."

Tucker jerked his shoulder away from Oliver's hand. "Dude, why are you acting like your grandfather?"

Oliver shrugged. "I have to. It's my legacy. You know my grandfather was Eggshell's first principal." He pointed at a framed picture of a man with glasses. He had the same green eyes as Oliver's and similar wavy hair. Only he was wrinkly and old looking. "Plus, I'm embarking on a career where the average age of a principal in this country is 49.3.

Behaving like an eleven-year-old will undoubtedly be unsuitable."

"Well, acting like you're forty-nine *point* three around us, is not cool," said Tucker.

Oliver laughed and shook his head. "No worries! It's going to be great to see you guys all the time again."

April Mae gave Tucker a skeptical glance. "I suppose."

"Sure, it will," said Tucker. "But it's still kind of weird that you're our principal now." He elbowed April Mae. "Right?"

April Mae held up her hand and studied her ring as it rapidly changed colors. "Not sure. Even my mood ring doesn't know how I should feel about this."

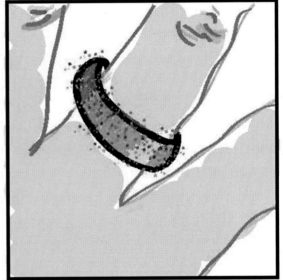

"Just like the trick for spelling principal correctly, remember that the principal is your pal, P-A-L." As soon as that came out of his mouth, Oliver knew how dorky it sounded and regretted saying it.

Tucker took a step back and held his palms in the air. "Yo, dude! The trick to being our pal is to not say stuff like that."

"Except that I don't think we're even allowed to be your pals now that you're the principal," said April Mae. She inspected her ring with a puzzled look on her face.

"But I didn't see anything in the principal's handbook prohibiting it," said Oliver.

"In that case, here," said Tucker, while pushing his sweatshirt sleeves up to his elbows. "Nothing up my sleeves..."

With a theatrical motion, he pulled a silk scarf from his back pocket and waved it. He then slid something out of his other pocket without April Mae or Oliver noticing.

"Ta da!" Tucker held up an envelope. "Here's an extra invitation to my birthday party." He extended it toward Oliver. "You should come."

April Mae grabbed one end just as Oliver grabbed the other end. They had a tug-of-war until she won.

"Are you crazy, Tuck?" she said. "This isn't the good old days. He's Principal Kidd now. He can't come to your party."

April Mae looked at her mood ring, changing colors once again. "Oh gosh. Maybe he should. I just don't know!" She held the invitation toward Tucker. "It's your party. You decide."

"Maybe I could just stop in?" asked Oliver.

Head bully, fifth-grader Elwood Lyons with his blonde buzz cut and chipped front tooth, butted in and grabbed the invitation. He tore open the envelope. "When is the party? I'll stop by, so you can share your birthday loot with me."

Tucker tossed down a handful of his magic trick rocks that exploded with a loud POP when they hit the floor. Thick purple smoke surrounded them. The kids gasped and waved the smoke around while Chelsea squawked.

When the purple smoke cleared, Elwood held up the envelope with a smirk.

"Nice try, Houdini, but I still have the invitation." Elwood looked in the envelope, looked on the floor, turned in a circle, then held the envelope upside down and shook it.

"Hey!" said Elwood. "Where did it go?"

Oliver held up the invitation with a smile before putting it in his pocket.

"It's back where it belongs," said Tucker.

"You got Tucked, Lyons," said April Mae.

Oliver nodded in agreement. "Tucked."

"Righteously Tucked," said Tucker. He felt proud that his magic trick pranks were so notorious that they had their own nickname.

Elwood glared at Tucker. "If I come to your party, it will be cool. If Principal Dweeb shows up, you'll be the laughing stock of the school." He crumpled the envelope and shook his fist before stomping off.

"You don't think he's right, do you?" asked Oliver. He still felt the sting of being called a dweeb. "About me..."

"Nah," said Tucker. "Not unless college turned you into an even bigger dweeb, Ollie. Oops. I mean Mr. Kidd."

April Mae and Tucker waved to Oliver as they headed down the hall when the bell rang.

Oliver pushed his glasses up higher on his nose and lifted Chelsea so she was eye level.

"I'm not a dweeb, am I, Chels?"

The chicken tilted her head and shrugged her wings. "Bok!"

"And I'm not really going to cause Tuck to become the laughing stock of the school, am I?"

"Squawk!"

"I was thinking that being friends with me would increase a student's social status. You know, having friends at the top and all." Oliver frowned. "Maybe April Mae was right. Maybe as the principal I can't be a friend to my old friends anymore. Oh, chicken feathers!"

"Squawk! *Squawk!*"

"Sorry. No offense, girl." Oliver scratched Chelsea's head until she nuzzled affectionately into his arm. "Well, no one will think I'm a dweeb after what I'm about to announce in my first assembly. Come on. Time to head to the auditorium."

Chapter

The school auditorium was packed with fidgety students and anxious looking teachers. Everyone was buzzing about Eggshell Elementary School having the world's first kid principal. And being that this was his first assembly on the first day of school, Oliver knew he should feel a little anxious. But being on stage was nothing new to him. He was quite used to accepting awards and giving speeches. Instead of nervously tossing himself about, his toaster tart was doing a happy dance!

Mr. Dagger was at the podium on stage. "And now, without further ado, here is your new principal – Oliver Kidd." He swept an outstretched arm in Oliver's direction.

During slow and polite clapping, Oliver dashed across the front row on his way to the stage. He was high-fiving and shaking hands with the students and some of the teachers.

Mr. Dagger sat next to Mrs. Indigo, the art teacher. She had short spiky aqua hair, wore peacock feather earrings, and paint-splattered overalls, and smelled like modeling clay.

"This child isn't going to last ten minutes in this job," said Mr. Dagger. "I might as will start moving my furniture into his office now."

"Don't count your chickens just yet," said Mrs. Indigo. "I remember Oliver Kidd as being very creative, years ago, in my class. I bet he'll have extremely innovative ideas for this school."

Meanwhile, up on stage, Oliver made several attempts to reach the microphone that Mr. Dagger left in a very high position. He couldn't stretch or jump high enough to grab it. Scanning the floor for something to stand on, he spotted Chelsea strutting about. Oliver scooped up the chicken and extended her toward the microphone.

"Help me out here, girl."

The chicken clamped her beak on the microphone and pulled it down within Oliver's reach.

Mr. Dagger rolled his eyes. "Innovative ideas? Oh, monkey flunder. Oliver Kidd can't finger paint his way through this job, Mrs. Indigo. Besides, that loco chicken would do better as principal than Kidd."

Everyone was startled into silence when Chelsea took the mike with a loud, "*Bok!*"

"Happy first day of school, everyone," said Oliver. "I'll keep this short and sweet. Studies have proven that fresh air and physical activity stimulate brain function. Soooo...who wants longer recess?"

The students stood to cheer and clap and whistle. The shocked teachers shushed them and motioned to sit.

"Wait, there's more," said Oliver. "Our schoolyard is now connected to Eggshell Chicken Farm and Spa. You can play with all the chickens outside too!"

More cheering students. More shocked teachers. Chelsea shook her butt around on stage, bobbing and clapping her wings.

Oliver held his palm out like a stop sign until everyone quieted down. "And you can forget that old rule about no gum in school. Since everyone loves to chew bubble gum, I am now allowing it." Oliver pulled a sack full of bubble gum from under the podium. He jumped off the stage and threw fistfuls out at his audience. The students cheered like crazy while reaching for the gum. They all shoved it in their mouths and blew bubbles, as fast as they could. The shocked teachers were turning a little green.

Back on stage, Oliver blew a big bubble that popped in his face. As he pulled it off his nose and cheeks, the students cheered louder. The teachers looked greener.

April Mae gave her mood ring a puzzled expression when it changed to red. She spit out her gum into the empty wrapper. "Boo! Boo!"

"Why are you booing?" asked Tucker. "You like bubble gum even more than you like Kevin Blake."

April Mae shrugged. "My ring turned red. That means I'm supposed to be mad."

Principal Kidd put Chelsea at the microphone to bok everyone to attention again.

"My next new rule: Since some kids will always run in the hallways, I'm allowing runners to pass walkers as long as the coast is clear."

There were louder cheers from the students. The shocked teachers looked around in silence.

April Mae's ring went from red to green and now changed to purple. This was all too confusing for her. She pouted and then cupped her hands around her mouth and shouted: "Boo! Terrible idea. Boo! Boo!"

Tucker elbowed her. "What's wrong with you? These ideas are so great that I bet I'll become the most popular kid in school by having him at my party!"

"I know," said April Mae. "But the problem is, my mood ring disagrees."

Chelsea did a silencing squawk, so Principal Kidd could finish the assembly.

"That's all the new school rules for now," said Oliver. "Have a great first day!"

The students were stomping, whistling and shouting their way out of the auditorium. Some blew giant gum bubbles while others ran past the slow walking kids, causing massive collisions. The teachers looked like dazed zombies.

Oliver ran down an empty hallway where a 'Wet Paint' sign hung. He felt happy enough to flip cartwheels. Except, he didn't know how to flip a cartwheel. being that academics had trumped gymnastics throughout his eleven years on earth.

Loud footsteps echoed down the hallway, followed by Mr. Dagger's booming voice.

"Kidd, have you gone crazy?"

Oliver stopped, turned and looked up. "Huh?"

"These new rules of yours," said Mr. Dagger. "Allowing running in the hallways? Bubble gum? Longer recess? Students playing with filthy chickens? It's craziness!"

"Squawk!" Chelsea pecked at his shoe.

Oliver held up his forefinger. "Hold that thought. I just need to check on one thing."

Oliver ran around the corner with Mr. Dagger closely following at his heels.

"Hang on," said Mr. Dagger. "I'm not done…"

While a painter put the finishing touches on a giant Eggshell logo on the wall, Mr. Dagger's jacket sleeve hooked onto the painter's utility belt. The sleeve ripped completely off. He grumbled as they both stumbled. Mr. Dagger landed faced down. The painter teetered off balance, trailing a line of white paint across Mr. Dagger's butt.

"Gob dash it," yelled Mr. Dagger. "This is my new suit!"

Oliver picked up the ripped jacket sleeve and held it toward the vice principal.

"Um, need a hand?" asked Oliver.

Mr. Dagger gritted his teeth. "No! Run along and go play principal." He motioned with his hand for Oliver to leave. "I'm fine."

After Oliver zoomed away, Mr. Dagger squatted next to Chelsea.

"You know, chicken, I'm not really fine. I'm really boiling mad. Principal Kidd's job should be mine, gob dash it!" Mr. Dagger stood and then bent down close to Chelsea's face. "And you're going to help me get it. It's time to show the health department how Principal Kidd's new rules violate every code in the book."

Chelsea's eyes widened. She shook her head no. "Bok! *Bok!*"

"Oh yes," said Mr. Dagger. "Starting with one of the biggest violations...*you*!"

Mr. Dagger lunged at Chelsea. She ran as fast as her little chicken legs would let her, zigzagging in an attempt to get away from the nasty vice principal.

Chapter

Chelsea rounded the corner and mingled her way in line with a group of second graders. Just when Mr. Dagger spotted her, the chicken ran outside to safety. when the recess bell rang and the back doors flew open.

Elwood Lyons pushed his way past the smaller kids, knocking some of them over, and then cupped his mouth and yelled out, "REEEEEECESS!"

Students ran everywhere. Some were on swings. Others were on the jungle gym. The chicken farm gates opened wide and chickens ran around all over the schoolyard with the kids. There was laughter, squeals, squawks, and feathers flying in the air.

Mr. Dagger ducked in his office and grabbed a basket filled with Super Duper bubble gum that was hidden in his closet. "This ought to cause some damage."

He brought it out to the schoolyard, found Oliver and handed him the basket. "I've confiscated these over the years. Now that you allow bubble gum, go pass them around. It just might make you popular, Kidd."

Oliver perked up at the thought of popularity. He had never achieved that before. "Stupendous idea. Thanks!"

Feeling confused, Elwood unwrapped the gum and gave Mr. Dagger a puzzled look. "Why are you helping that annoying little know-it-all to score brownie points with everyone?"

Mr. Dagger took the gum out of Elwood's hand and held it up.

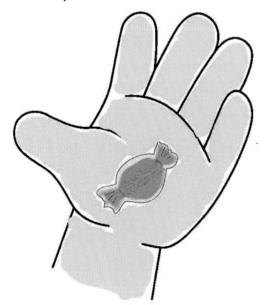

"Just watch what happens to Super Duper bubble gum when it's way past the expiration date." His grin spread across his face. "Help me out with my plan, Elwood, and I'll help you out."

"Help you how?"

Mr. Dagger took his cell phone out and

pointed to the right. "You and I are going to roam around the schoolyard and shoot some video with our phones. Easy, right?"

Elwood nodded. "Sure. But how are you going help *me* out?"

"I'll fix it so you don't get detention this entire month," said Mr. Dagger.

"For the next three months."

"Two."

"Two and a half," countered Elwood.

"Half a month.," said Mr. Dagger.

"One month," said Elwood, with his hands folded across his chest.

"You drive a hard bargain," said Mr. Dagger. "One month it is."

The two shook hands and headed in opposite directions.

When Elwood reached the kickball field, he couldn't believe his eyes. Everyone was making faces and spitting the gum out. Kids all over were gagging and complaining.

"Yuck! This tastes disgusting!"

"Eww! This gum is horrible!"

"Blaaaaah!"

Elwood took his phone out and hit 'record' on the video feature. The sticky gum was stretching like taffy between the ground and the bottoms of shoes. The kickball pitcher's fingers got stuck to the ball and the game had to stop. He got it all on video. Even some of the things the kids were saying:

"Aww. Now we can't play anymore, either."

"This is the worst recess ever!"

"Why did Principal Kidd give us this awful stuff?"

"I don't know," said Elwood. "Let's go find him."

He spotted Principal Kidd near a group of first graders by the jungle gym. The smaller students were blowing bubbles so large they were being lifted off the ground.

"Whoa," said Elwood. "Cool!"

"This is *not* cool," said Oliver. He jumped up and popped a bunch of bubbles before anyone could float away. "Chelsea, take over down here," he said to the bird. "We can't let anyone disappear into space." Oliver's voice sounded an octave higher as sheer panic ran through him.

Chelsea and her chicken friends hopped as high as they could. The birds punctured the bubbles with their beaks so the students could land on the ground.

Oliver grabbed a megaphone and climbed quickly to the top of the jungle gym. "Attention! Recess is ending early. Everyone back inside, immediately!"

While all the students shuffled slowly back into the school groaning and complaining, Oliver spotted a girl attached to a giant gum bubble as she floated past him. He jumped off the jungle gym and grabbed her around the waist. When they landed on the ground, he popped the bubble.

Bringing the megaphone back to his mouth, he added, "And bubble gum is strictly prohibited until further notice."

"Way to go, bro," said Tucker on his way past Oliver. "This was the worst recess in the history of recesses."

"I agree," said April Mae. She looked at her mood ring. "Hmm. On second thought, it wasn't all that bad." The ring changed colors again. "Actually, it was a pretty awesome time!"

"You don't have to pretend, April Mae," said Oliver. "I know it was awful. Trust me, I feel worse than you about it. But I'll make sure the rest of the day is great."

Tucker fist-bumped Oliver. "Counting on it."

Oliver had no idea if he really could make good on his promise. He wished he could float away on a giant bubble right then and there. Would the rest of the day really take a turn and become great, or would he mess things up like he had for recess?

Chapter

Elwood was called down to Vice Principal Dagger's office. Nothing new. Only this time, he knew he wasn't in any trouble. This time was going to be a fun visit.

Mr. Dagger was playing back the video he had shot on his phone during recess. "This is great! Let's see what you've got, Elwood."

The two of them sat with their heads together watching the videos, laughing hysterically.

"Look at that kid," said Elwood, about a boy who was so completely trapped by the sticky bubble gum that he had to take off and abandon his sneakers.

"And that one," said Mr. Dagger. They watched a girl running in circles, spitting out the gum and crying. "I suppose I shouldn't be laughing at her like this."

"You're right," said Elwood. "You should be laughing at this one instead. Check it out!" He pointed to the video and they both busted out in laughter as five floating first graders got their bubbles stuck and formed what looked like a hot air balloon.

Mr. Dagger typed an e-mail, attached the video and hit 'send'. "This ought to get the health inspector's attention."

He turned to Elwood and grinned. "The faster we can prove that Kidd's idiotic new rules are bad for the school, the faster I can take over as principal."

"Yeah," said Elwood. "Principal Punk has got to go. He's stealing all my thunder. It's *my* job to cause scenes around here. Let's get rid of this guy!"

Chapter

Oliver sat slumped in his chair, while Chelsea was perched on his desk.

"What just happened out there?" asked Oliver. He started sweating just thinking about recess. Oliver pointed to the computer. "See if Super Duper bubble gum has been reformulated recently, girl."

Chelsea pecked away at the keyboard and hit enter. They both read through articles about bubble gum on the computer screen.

"Hmm," said Oliver. "Similar oddities have occurred with gum significantly past its expiration date." He frowned. "This was a bonehead move for a genius. I should have done my research before handing out anything to the students. These kids are counting on me for everything." Oliver sighed. "Geez, there certainly is a whole lot involved with this principal gig."

Chelsea nodded in agreement.

April Mae gave a knock and poked her head in the doorway.

Oliver waved her in.

"Close call with that bubble gum debacle, huh?" said Oliver. "And to think, I was going to make goody bags filled with them for Tuck's birthday party."

April Mae looked down at her sandals. "Um, about the party." She shifted from side to side, trying to figure out if there was a nice way to say what she needed to say. "Everyone agrees you ruined recess, and pretty much the whole first day of school. So, um...Tucker's afraid no one will come to his party if you're there."

"Oh," said Oliver. It felt as if a giant petrified gum wad landed in his stomach, with a thud. "Guess he's afraid to tell me himself, huh? And you won't go if I'm there either, April Mae?"

April Mae held up her hand, watching her ring in hopes of the right answer. It just kept changing colors. Frustrated, she shook her head. "I just don't know," she said. "This stupid ring still isn't working." Her stomach grumbled. "And it was no help to me when I tried to order lunch today in the cafeteria. I couldn't make up my mind in time and I'm starving now!"

Oliver handed her a granola bar he grabbed from his desk drawer.

"Thanks," she said. April Mae took a big bite before continuing. "Then Kevin Blake asked if I would be at Tuck's party and I thought my ring signaled to be cool, so I told him it was none of his business!"

Oliver had budget reports, bus schedules, classroom work plans, core curriculum, fifteen e-mails, and twenty phone messages to review. It was all making his head spin. But April Mae was clearly upset. He knew she needed his attention first.

"Why don't you tell Kevin you were just kidding," he suggested. "Let him know you'll be at the party and you'll save a dance for him, if he comes."

April Mae laughed. "You sounded like your grandfather again, Ollie – I mean, Mr. Kidd." She put her hands behind her back. "And I'm not going to consult my ring because I know that's a great idea." She turned around and gave a quick peek to her ring, nonetheless.

Before leaving, April Mae dropped an envelope in Chelsea's nest, next to Principal Kidd's in-basket. She blocked his view so only the chicken saw the delivery.

Chelsea held the envelope down with one foot and ripped it open with her beak. After reading it, the chicken flung her body on top of it to hide it from Oliver.

Oliver tilted his head, in an attempt to read some of it. "What is it, girl? What are you hiding?"

Chelsea considered pretending that she laid an egg and had to remain there, but knew she couldn't cover this up forever. She shifted to one side and hid her face with one wing.

Oliver read Chelsea's mail. "Oh great. *You* get an invitation to Tuck's party and I'm uninvited!"

The chicken blushed and shrugged. "Bok! Bok!"

Oliver could think of only one person who might be able to help him through this kooky predicament.

Chapter

Oliver entered the office of hard-of-hearing guidance counselor, Mrs. Winnie Huggswell. She was the school's oldest employee who was somewhere between 65 and 99 years old, no one knew for sure. She was round with spare chins, and eyes that twinkled and crinkled when she smiled. She passed Oliver a plate of the best smelling homemade cookies.

Mrs. Huggswell looked into Oliver's eyes with concern. "What's troubling you, dear?"

"I was uninvited to Tucker's party," he said. "Even Chelsea's going!"

Confused, Mrs. Huggswell looked out the window. "What? It's snowing?"

"No, wish I was *going* to the party," said Oliver, speaking a bit louder now. He slouched in his chair and pouted. "Sometimes I just want to be one of the guys."

"Oh, a disguise."

Mrs. Huggswell rummaged through a bin of dress-up clothes and accessories, and handed Oliver a fake mustache and a hat. "Here, try this on."

Oliver put on the shiny gold hat. He looked at himself from several angles in the mirror on the wall.

"Not too sure about this gold hat."

"Don't call me an old bat!"

"No," he said. "You've confused my words!"

"What? My cookies taste like turds?"

Oliver shoved several cookies in his mouth at once. He spewed out crumbs while talking with his mouth full. "No, see? I *love* your cookies."

Mrs. Huggswell smiled. She put the cookies in a bag and handed them to Oliver.

"Good. I'm glad," she said. "Take the rest. They'll help you make new friends."

Oliver sighed and then screamed out, "Great idea. Thanks!"

Mrs. Huggswell pressed her palms against her ears and scrunched up her face.

"No need to shout at me, dear."

Oliver gathered the disguises and cookies before waving goodbye. On his way back to his office, he felt confident that he could handle anything.

That confidence washed away when he saw who was waiting for him in his office.

Chapter

Waiting in his office, Oliver found Mr. Dagger with a strange little balding man, wearing white gloves and holding a clipboard. The man was wiping one of the bookcases with a handkerchief. Oddly, the room had taken on the scent of lemon furniture polish.

"Several complaints were lodged," said Mr. Dagger, "so the health inspector needs to look around."

"I'm Inspector Dusty," said the man, holding out his gloved hand to shake Oliver's. He spoke with a lisp and spit whenever he said any "S's" He used his handkerchief to wipe up, leaving everything with a spit shine. "I'm afraid I have bad news, son. Very bad news." Spit. Wipe.

Oliver narrowly dodged Inspector Dusty's spit spray. He scooted to the other side of his desk to distance himself before more S's were spoken.

"I've spotted several safety code violations," sprayed the inspector. He wiped the desk clean and then tore a sheet from his clipboard. He slapped a violation down on the desk.

"Chickens on premises," said Inspector Dusty.

A shaking and cowering Chelsea hid herself behind Oliver.

"Students running in the hallways," said the inspector. Wipe. Tear. Slap. "Raw eggs everywhere." Wipe. Tear. Slap. "And potentially dangerous bubble gum."

Just when Inspector Dusty wiped his spittle, tore the last violation off his pad and slapped it down on the pile, Oliver had blown a gigantic bubble with his own gum.

Oliver's eyes grew wide. He quickly ducked under his desk and Chelsea popped it with her beak. She then neatly deposited the wad in the garbage can.

"You have 24-hours to fix it all," said the inspector, "or I shut this school down."

Inspector Dusty wiped the last of his spit, then turned and left.

Needing to walk off his stress, a grownup trait Oliver learned from his grandfather, he began pacing. He felt like the walls were closing in on him and it was hard to take deep breaths.

The minute the principal's chair was vacant, Mr. Dagger slunk into it and put his feet up on the desk.

Oliver finally spoke, pacing even faster now. "This won't look at all suitable on my resume, if the school closes two days after I've become principal."

"Face it, Kidd," said Mr. Dagger, "you're in over your head. You need my help."

Oliver stopped and faced the vice principal. "What do you have in mind?"

"I'll take care of all these problems," said Mr. Dagger. "All you have to do is..."

"What?" yelped Oliver. "I'm ready to do anything!"

Mr. Dagger stood and looked down at Oliver. "Resign tomorrow and announce to the entire school that I will take your place, as principal."

Chapter

Oliver kept Mr. Dagger's suggestion to himself all day. If his parents found out, they would make a big stink. His mom would want to call Mr. Dagger and that would make Oliver seem like a little baby. He had to handle this himself. Besides, it was time for some fun. Tucker's birthday party had already started and Oliver was determined to go. He had a foolproof plan.

Hiding his bike in the bushes at Tuck's house, Oliver peered through the leaves. The party was in full swing with kids laughing, talking, dancing, music, balloons – and a few chickens. Lights twinkled from the tree branches. He could smell pizza, cheese puffs, and cupcakes. Oliver couldn't wait to get inside the backyard. This looked almost as much fun as quantum physics!

Oliver put on a hat, fake mustache and a trench coat. He took a giant pillowcase stuffed with cookies and flung it over his shoulder. It looked like Santa's toy sack.

The first person Oliver spotted was April Mae, pouring herself a soda by the food and drink table. Chelsea was at her feet pecking crumbs off the ground. Oliver crept along the bushes, getting closer.

April Mae's current crush, the cute and confident Kevin Blake, sauntered over. He was bopping to the music. "You ready for that dance now?"

April Mae examined her mood ring, still on the fritz. She pouted and then gulped down more soda instead of answering.

Oliver popped out of the bushes, reached into the sack and handed them each a goody bag filled with cookies. He spoke in a strange accent. "Here. Have cookie."

"You go to Eggshell?" asked Kevin. "Never seen you around."

April Mae eyed Mustache Man suspiciously while munching her cookie. "You look very familiar," she said.

Chelsea squawked and nodded her head in agreement.

"Exchange student," said Oliver. "New to country."

"With a 'stash?" asked Kevin. "Dude, fifth graders don't have that much facial hair!"

Oliver stroked his fake mustache. "Trouble with English. Held back."

April Mae waved her half- eaten cookie in the air. "These taste *very* familiar."

Chelsea bobbed over and April Mae fed the chicken a piece of the cookie. Chelsea puffed out her belly and held her wings to the sides of her head, then squawked loudly.

Chelsea's clue suddenly clicked for April Mae. She felt like she had just locked together two puzzle pieces. "You're right, Chels. These are Mrs. Huggswell's cookies!"

Bored with this whole debate, Kevin wanted to get back to business. "So, did you want to dance or what?"

Chelsea bopped around happily, shaking her booty, squawking and flapping her wings.

"Not *you*," said Kevin. "I meant April Mae."

Chelsea folded her wings over her chest and looked angry.

April Mae consulted her ring again, hoping it would tell her to go for it.

"But, um, my ring says..."

Kevin adjusted the bandana on his head. "Never mind. My doo rag says it's time to go." He rolled his eyes and left.

Elwood Lyons showed up, scanned Oliver's disguise from head to toe and laughed out loud.

Tucker rushed over when he heard Elwood's cackle. "What are *you* doing here?" he asked the party-crashing bully.

"Never mind me," said Elwood. "What's *he* doing here?" He pulled the mustache off Oliver.

Tucker couldn't believe his eyes. This was not good. This could ruin his whole party *and* social rank, for the next decade. He yanked the tablecloth, leaving all the drinks and food in place. With a wave of the tablecloth, he covered both Oliver and Elwood with it. Everyone stopped dancing and talking. They gathered closer to watch.

Chelsea tugged the cord to unplug all the outdoor lights.

When everything became dark, Tucker whispered to Oliver. "If everyone sees it's you they'll hate both of us, so *run!*"After Oliver ran off, Tucker put the lights back on. "Now that I have your attention," he said, "it's time for some magic. Taadaa!" He pulled the tablecloth away, revealing a stunned Elwood Lyons, wearing the fake

mustache, and with Chelsea perched on his head.

The party guests cheered and clapped then all shouted out, "Tucked! Tucked! He got Tucked!"

Once Oliver was home, he was glad he hadn't ruined things for Tucker. But what would happen tomorrow? The school might get shut down if Oliver didn't fix things quick. That would ruin his career. Ruin his legacy. Ruin the education of hundreds of students. Ruin jobs for the teachers. Even ruin all those extra places for Chelsea to poop. He had to make things right!

Chapter

The next morning at school, while April Mae and Tucker were walking down the hallway, the school secretary, Miss Happ, made an announcement over the PA.

Miss Happ's cheerful voice boomed from every speaker: "There will be an emergency assembly at two o'clock today. Everyone must attend. Have a hap, hap, happy day!"

Tucker and April Mae looked at each other and without uttering a word, turned around and ran toward the main entrance. They arrived at the principal's office out of breath.

"Yo, why the emergency assembly?" Tucker asked Principal Kidd.

"Yeah," said April Mae. "What's going on?"

"I've messed up big time," said Oliver. He shut his office door and then whispered, "This is totally confidential, but I need to resign and name Mr. Dagger as principal."

"*What?*" asked Tucker. "That's craziness. So, you ruined recess. Big deal. And it wasn't chill to crash my party in a disguise. We won't tell anyone about that. But, hey, that doesn't mean you need to quit your job over it."

Oliver felt like jumping up and down for joy but knew that wouldn't be at all cool. "You mean you want me to stay here as the principal?"

"Not necessarily," said April Mae. "But it sure would beat having Mr. Dagger in charge."

"Oh," said Oliver. "There may be no choice anyway. Health Inspector Dusty is arriving after lunch and expects to see viable solutions to all the health and safety violations. I haven't quite worked it all out yet."

"Between your genius mind," said April Mae, "and our regular ones, we'll figure out a solution. We need you here. Let's do this!"

Oliver and Tucker just stared at April Mae. She inspected herself and looked puzzled. "What? Is something on me? Why are you staring like that?"

Oliver spoke first. "You were so assertive and gave specific directions without consulting your..."

"...your mood ring," said Tucker. "Where is it?"

April Mae smiled and flipped her thick braid around to the front of her shoulder. The sparkling ring was attached to the end of her braid.

"While I was reading this morning's horoscope," she said, "I felt a clear sign that it was best to use the mood ring as a hair accessory, instead. Best decision I've ever made."

"Couldn't agree more," said Oliver. "Now let's figure out how to fix everything around here." He tapped away on the keyboard and turned the computer monitor to face the others. "Here's the report I started."

April Mae, Tucker and Chelsea huddled around Oliver, as he spread out all the health and safety violations on his desk.

April Mae pointed to one. "This is an easy fix. Just cook 'em."

"And for this one," said Tucker, "we can make some magic in the art room."

Oliver held up one of the violations. "An unfortunate incident that involved white paint and the back of Mr. Dagger's pants has given me an idea for this one."

Oliver stood, pushed his glasses up, straightened his tie and smiled. "Thanks, I've got it from here. Time for you two to get back to class."

Oliver raced out of his office, anxious to get his new plans in place. But would he have enough time to pull it all off, before Inspector Dusty arrived?

Chapter

Later that afternoon, a proud and beaming Oliver Kidd was showing Inspector Dusty around the school. Inspector Dusty nodded and took notes on his clipboard, as Oliver pointed out lanes that had been painted on both sides of

the hallway floors. FAST was painted along the left lanes and SLOW on the right lanes.

"No more collisions," said Oliver. "There are now fast lanes for the runners to safely pass the walkers."

Three running students zoomed past them, utilizing the fast lane. Oliver and Inspector Dusty then walked briskly on the left, to pass a pack of slow moving kindergarten kids.

"Smart thinking, Principal Kidd," sprayed the inspector.

Chelsea skidding skidded across one of the spit puddles and then wiped it dry with one of her wings.

Next, Oliver brought Inspector Dusty out to the playground. He pointed to a teacher with a chicken on her lap. She was surrounded by a group of students sitting on the grass.

"By keeping the school and the chicken farm connected," explained Oliver, "we now offer hands-on farm and agricultural studies."

The two walked closer to the group and listened, as the teacher continued her lesson. "A hen will lay an average of 300 eggs per year," she said. She held up an egg.

When Oliver and Inspector Dusty made their way to the cafeteria's warm and steamy kitchen, a cook was holding up an egg. The room smelled like bacon and cheese. Students sat at a table with bowls and measuring cups. They watched the cook crack and scramble the egg, then did the same.

"All the eggs will be gathered daily," said Oliver, "and used as part of our new culinary arts program."

Inspector Dusty nodded and smiled. "Very nice, very nice! Looks tasty."

Chelsea blocked his flying spit from the S's with her wing to protect the food on the table.

Next stop was the art room. A poster of a face blowing a gum bubble was in the corner. Below it, was a table with a mound of molded chunks of chewed up bubble gum.

Oliver gestured to the corner. "This is our designated gum chewing area. The students must deposit their ABC gum here before leaving."

"ABC gum?" asked Inspector Dusty.

"Already Been Chewed," replied Oliver.

Mrs. Indigo joined them and pointed to the mound of gum on the table. "Our goal is to create the world's largest bubble gum sculpture. We want to beat the current world record!"

The health inspector made a face at the art teacher. "Hmm. Seems somewhat unsanitary."

Oliver brought over a bottle of hand sanitizer from Mrs. Indigo's desk but Inspector Dusty shook his head no. "I'm afraid this is still a violation."

"Oh no," said Mrs. Indigo. "But the kids love this. It's their favorite spot!"

Oliver had to think fast. He'd come this far. If he took away all the fun stuff, the students would hate him. He also couldn't let this one last violation shut down the school.

Chapter

It was time for the 2:00 assembly. As the students and teachers took their seats, everyone was murmuring, trying to guess what the emergency was all about. One student whispered in the ear of the person next to him, like the game 'telephone'. "I heard Principal Kidd is going to quit. Pass it on..."

The students continuing whispering down the row, passing the message.

"Principal Kidd just ate bad squid..."

"Principal Kidd eats bad kids for lunch..."

"Principal Kidd got punched for eating..."

"Principal Kidd's heart stopped beating!"

That last line was whispered to Mrs. Huggswell, who stood up all alarmed. She shouted toward the stage. "Oliver Kidd, you're going to quit?"

Oliver rushed to the podium on stage and had Chelsea squawk into the microphone, to quiet the crowd down.

"Those were my original plans," said Oliver. "But I'm no quitter. My grandfather was Eggshell's first principal. I'm not going to let him down. Or any of you down. Or myself either. I'm staying right here as principal!"

Mrs. Huggswell was beaming. She had put on that shiny gold hat from the dress-up bin and tipped it at Oliver.

Mrs. Indigo blew a big bubble with her gum while giving a thumbs-up. She couldn't get over how Oliver got rid of that last violation. He told the health inspector the gum sculpture had been named The Dusty. Mrs. Indigo had added that they named it after the Inspector since he had helped them all think outside of the box. Inspector Dusty

was so honored, he came up with the solution to move the table, with his statue, next to the sink for hand washing purposes. Then he had torn up the last violation.

Oliver continued speaking., "Our school failed the Safety Code inspection yesterday," he said, "because of my new rules. But…" He held up a sheet of paper with a big red P on it. "Today we passed! Eggshell Elementary School can remain open!"

The crowd cheered and clapped.

April Mae and Tucker were high-fiving and smiling.

Elwood Lyons was grimacing, while Mr. Dagger turned purple and gritted his teeth.

The students and teachers were still cheering after Principal Kidd dismissed everyone.

Elwood rushed over and sat next to Mr. Dagger. "This stinks worse than the chicken coop out back. I thought your plan was going to get rid of Principal Kidd, not make him more popular."

"Oh relax, gob dash it!" said Mr. Dagger. "I've got more tricks up my sleeve than just some old bubble gum."

Tucker was walking past just then and stopped. He reached behind Mr. Dagger's ear and pulled out a piece of Super Duper bubble gum and offered it to the vice principal.

"Did you say bubble gum?"

Mr. Dagger patted and probed both of his ears. "What the...?" He glared at Tucker.

Elwood Lyons rolled his eyes. "What a dumb trick."

"Guess I'll have to keep practicing other tricks then," said Tucker. "Because just like Principal Kidd, I'm not a quitter."

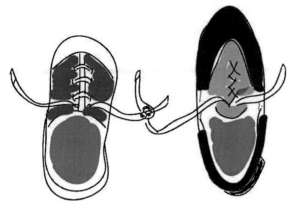

Mr. Dagger and Elwood stood to leave without realizing that Elwood's left sneaker laces had been tied to Mr. Dagger's right shoelaces. They both fell backwards with their tied feet up in the air.

April Mae thrust her fist up in the air. "Tucked!"

"Righteously Tucked!" Tucker picked up Chelsea and they headed out of the auditorium. He whispered to the chicken, "Nice job, girl."

When they reached the front of the school, kids were boarding the buses to head home. Tucker shouted out, "Leftover cupcakes at my house!"

April Mae rubbed her stomach. "Yum!" She waved at Kevin before he got on his bus. "You're meeting us there, right, Kev?"

"Are you sure you want me to?" he asked.

"Absolutely!" she said.

"Okay," said Kevin. "Meet you there in ten with some of the other kids."

"Sounds like fun, Tuck," said Oliver. "May I come?"

"Sure," said Tucker with a shrug. "And you won't need a disguise this time."

Mr. Dagger barged in, his scowl had deepened. "Principals are not permitted to socialize with students outside of school. It would show favoritism."

The three children looked at each other, not knowing what to say.

"Not even for one little cupcake?" asked Oliver.

Mr. Dagger shook his head. "Not even one little crumb. No can do. It's against the rules. And you know how *that* goes."

Oliver's head hung low. Not only was he missing out on yummy baked treats, but the opportunity to hang out with kids his own age. Something he seldom did, while rocketing through the prodigy program and accelerated college courses. He couldn't even look into his friends' eyes when he spoke. "Oh well. Have fun."

"Hang on." Mr. Dagger held up a forefinger. "There might be a way around this, Kidd."

Oliver felt like tickly sparklers went off in his belly. "What? How?"

"You go back to college for another degree," said Mr. Dagger, "while I run things around here. Then you'll be free to be a kid. You love going to school. You can see your friends and have fun after your classes. It's a win-win."

Tucker, April Mae and Chelsea stood behind Mr. Dagger shaking their heads no and wildly waving their hands and wings.

Oliver smiled. "What a kind offer, Mr. Dagger..."

April Mae and Tucker gasped. Chelsea squawked.

"But I want to be the best principal Eggshell's ever had," said Oliver. "You heard me in today's assembly, I'm no quitter! Plus, I promised my grandpa that my picture would hang next to his one day soon."

"Suit yourself, Kidd," said Mr. Dagger. "But don't come crying to me when you mess things up again."

After Mr. Dagger stormed off, April Mae hugged Oliver. Then Tucker and Oliver did their special handshake.

"Hold out your hand, Ollie," said Tucker. "I mean, Mr. Kidd."

Tucker covered Oliver's hand with a silk scarf and then twirled the scarf. "Abracadabra!" He pulled the scarf away and a birthday cupcake appeared in Oliver's palm.

Oliver felt thrilled for a second, but felt his smile droop when he realized his friends—no, make that his students— were about to leave without him.

"Well, time to get on the bus now, students," said Oliver. "Thanks for everything."

"You got it, Mr. Kidd," said Tucker.

"Bye, Principal Kidd," said April Mae.

As April Mae and Tucker waved goodbye from the bus window, Oliver and Chelsea sat on the steps of the front entrance. He shared his cupcake with the chicken.

"At least I'm still just plain ole Ollie to you. This school still rules, especially with you by my side, right, girl?"

Chelsea nuzzled next to him and rested her head on his arm. Then she stretched out a wing and put it around his shoulder.

"Squawk!"

About the Author

My mom used to tape paper to the tray on my highchair and give me crayons, so I've been drawing since before I can remember! I grew up in Elizabeth, NJ. That home had the coolest built-in bookcases jam packed with books. My mother taught in elementary school. I was raised loving books. My dad was a police detective. Not surprisingly, my favorite books as a child were the Nancy Drew mysteries.

I have a degree in art from Syracuse University. Most of my career years have been in advertising. From Madison Avenue to St. Petersburg, FL. Rockefeller Center and the Time-Life building will always be special to me. It's where I met my husband of 27-years, Dan.

I began reading to my son when I was pregnant. It led me to writing children's books from home. I'm a member of the Society of Children's Book Writers and Illustrators (SCBWI).

I had the unique opportunity to be selected to work with award-winning, kid-lit superstar, Jerry Spinelli, during a weeklong Highlights writer's workshop in 2006. What an honor! A workshop that week, sparked an idea for an article for FACES magazine. It turned into a monthly feature called "Dear Tommy" that ran for over seven years. I've also written for other children's magazines such as Fun For Kidz, Appleseeds and Highlights.

I tend to "think visually", often picturing my stories as TV shows or movies. So, I've taken TV Screenwriting classes in Alan Kingsberg's Advanced Writer Room in New York City. I hope to develop my chapter books into animation one day. If you are going to dream, you may as well ***DREAM BIG***!

I'm thrilled to now be part of the Foundations Books family, where my dreams are beginning to come true.

Acknowledgements

None of this would have been possible without the love, faith, strength, help, and support from my husband of 27-years, Danny Colón and son, Tommy. I love you both so much – even on all those days I would yell to be quiet and leave me alone while I wrote! Thank you to my talented artist sis, Roe Murray for encouraging me to use my artwork for this book and for all your prayers. My childhood friends from New Jersey (I shall not name names to protect the innocent!) – you all still make me laugh! My various critique groups – your help is priceless. Thank you to educators everywhere, especially art teacher Dr. George Trogler and TV screenwriting teacher, Alan Kingsberg. Laurie Calkhoven, thanks for so many years of fun, and for getting me through my first SCBWI conference in New York City – I was so nervous! The entire New Jersey chapter of SCBWI – you have gotten me through so much and made me stay in this often crazy and frustrating business. Kathy Temean, who led the group for so many years and got me involved in volunteering. The New Jersey chapter is "my tribe." Sheri Oshins, who not only has made me laugh so hard I thought I would die, she also had the good sense to help me during a faculty dinner and she literally saved my life during a crazy, out of the blue stroke! Kim, Annie, Cathy, Leeza, Linda (and anyone else I missed) thanks for being there for me. My new SCBWI tribe in Florida, thank you for your warm, Southern hospitality. To every creative soul who had the guts to put their work out into this world - you have all influenced me. To anyone who ever gave me a negative critique or chipped away at my self-confidence, thank you for adding to my determination to show you that I can do this! A huge thank you to Laura Ranger, Steve Soderquist, Toni Michelle, and the rest of the Foundations Books family for bringing my characters into the world. Lastly, thank you to my loving parents, now promoted to guardian angels, for bringing me into the world and allowing me to be creative. I am a bit of a late bloomer, so a huge thanks to God for being so patient with me as I took many years to finally use the gifts I had been given.

Thank you to all the young people who will take the time to read this book. Happy reading, make the most of school, and dream big!

Principal Kidd: School Rules

WE WANT TO HEAR FROM YOU...

TRY TO WIN THE "NEW RULE" CONTEST!
(no purchase necessary)

Principal Kidd announced several new rules for Eggshell Elementary School and he will be announcing more in future books.

If you were the principal of your school right now, what new rule would you put in place and why?

Send us your answer along with your name, age, address, phone number and email address.
(Please get parent/guardian permission, include their name.)

If we choose your new rule as the winner, you will:

- Have your name in a special acknowledgement section of an upcoming book in the PRINCIPAL KIDD series by Connie T. Colon
- Your new rule will be part of the story
- Receive a free autographed copy of the book

Winner will be selected by author and publisher.

Please email your entry to: Connie@FoundationsBooks.net or www.conniecolon.com

Or

Mail to: Foundations, LLC
105 Carries Cove
Brandon, MS 39047

GOOD LUCK!!!

Other Children's Titles From Foundations Books
www.FoundationsBooks.net

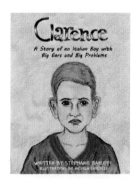

Clarence
By Stephanie Baruffi

A story of an Italian boy with big ears
and a big family.

Easy Peasey, Learning is Easy
By Alissa B. Gregory

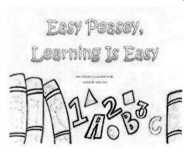

Fun, colorful book to help
children learn, their
alphabet, colors, numbers
and shapes.

School's Not So Bad
By Alissa B. Gregory

Go along with Mary Ellen on her
first day of school, to discover
school's not so bad.

Made in the USA
Middletown, DE
19 March 2017